To Peggy

First published in hardback in Great Britain by HarperCollins Children's Books in 2008

1 3 5 7 9 10 8 6 4 2
ISBN-13: 978-0-00-726946-4
ISBN-10: 0-00-726946-3

HarperCollins Children's Books is a division of HarperCollins Publishers Ltd.

Text copyright © Michael Bond 2008
Illustrations copyright © Peggy Fortnum and William Collins Sons and Co. Ltd
1958, 1959, 1960, 1961, 1962, 1964, 1968, 1970
Printed and bound in Hong Kong

For more Paddington fun visit: www.paddington50th.com

MICHAEL BOND

Paddington

My Book of
Marmalade

With illustrations by PEGGY FORTNUM

HarperCollins *Children's Books*

𝒜 note from 𝒫addington

I was brought up in Darkest Peru, and when I was small I was given marmalade chunks to eat. Because I didn't have any teeth at the time I could make one chunk last for several days. It's called 'eking'.

My Aunt Lucy often says, 'A spoonful of marmalade a day keeps the doctor at bay,' and she should know.

She's one of the oldest inhabitants of the Home for Retired Bears in Lima.

If you think you would like to learn more about marmalade, read on.

Marmalade Memories

*W*hen my Aunt Lucy sent me off as a stowaway on a big ocean liner in search of a better life, she gave me a jar of marmalade for the voyage. I made it last all the way to England. If I hadn't known how to eke out the chunks I might never have ended up on Paddington station in London – which is how I got my name. And I certainly wouldn't be living at number 32 Windsor Gardens with a nice family like the Browns. That's another reason why marmalade means so much to me.

Soon after I arrived, the Browns took me to a very grand restaurant for a treat. I had a bath specially, but when I got there I found the menu was all in French and I didn't know what to order.

The man in charge said there was nothing they didn't have, so I ordered a marmalade sandwich with custard.

I don't think the chef had ever been asked for one of those before. He came out of his kitchen and looked straight at me. But I gave him one of my hard stares and so that was the last we saw of him!

$\mathcal{A}$nother of Aunt Lucy's sayings is, 'It's a wise bear who knows where his next marmalade sandwich is coming from.'

That's why I never go anywhere without having one under my hat.

I'm surprised more people don't do it. I suppose it's because not many wear a hat these days, which is a pity. It's got me out of trouble quite a few times.

I once had a temporary job in a barber's shop. I was left on my own and I found myself having to cut a customer's hair using electric clippers.

They ran amok and before I knew where I was, the top of his head looked like a map of the underground.

Luckily he had dozed off, so I tried gluing it back on. But I do wish now I had used marmalade, because it would have scrubbed off…

The other day, I saw a jar of marmalade with 'By Royal Appointment' on the label. It made me wonder if the Queen keeps a marmalade sandwich under her crown when she goes out. I would if it was me and I was opening Parliament.

It would be a long time to go without otherwise. She might even have one in the palm of her hand when she's waving to the crowd. I saw a programme about magic on television showing how it's done. They said the quickness of the hand deceives the eye. It's probably why she always wears white gloves.

$\mathcal{A}$nother time I was in a crowded lift in Barkridges and a lady rested a heavy shopping basket on my head while we were going down.

I was wondering why it was so quiet when a man standing next to me asked if I knew I had marmalade running down over my ears.

He got off at the next floor and by the time we reached the bargain basement everyone else had gone too.

It set me wondering about where marmalade came from in the first place and I knew just the person to ask; my best friend, Mr Gruber.

Marmalade – A Potted History

$\mathcal{M}$r Gruber has an antique shop in Portobello Road and most mornings we have our elevenses together.

He says marmalade can be traced all the way back to Greece thousands of years ago, when someone chopped open a quince to see what was inside. Whoever it was, he probably wished he hadn't, because although quince looks like an apple, the outside is very hard and the inside tastes very sharp.

When I told Mrs Bird, she said she can sometimes trace marmalade all the way back to my bedroom.

$\mathcal{M}$r Gruber thinks his man probably tried boiling the quince to soften the skin, adding honey to sweeten it.

If he did, he would have made a discovery. As soon as the pot was removed from the heat, the liquid would have started to gel.

That was because quince is full of a chemical called *pectin*, which reacts with the sugar in honey, causing it to set.

I'm glad our cocoa isn't full of pectin, otherwise Mr Gruber and I would have to drink it very quickly. I wouldn't fancy having it setting inside me on the way home.

$\mathcal{A}$nother thing I learnt
from Mr Gruber was
that in those days if he
had wanted to keep the
fruit, the usual method
was to leave it in the sun
to dry. However, as the
mixture had already begun to

set he would most likely have put it
into an open container until it turned into
a paste. The Greek word for the paste was *melimelon*.

I tried to get a jar of it for Mrs Bird at the cut-price
grocer's in the market, but the man said they were waiting
for some to come in.

*I*n the meantime, other countries were also taking an interest in quince. Arab dishes of the day often made use of it, and over 2000 years ago, Apicius, author of the first Roman cookery book, knowing his fellow countrymen disliked having their meat served plain, added it to his recipe for roast veal.

$\mathcal{M}$r Gruber says that a milestone in the history of marmalade took place in the 10th century, when the Arabs introduced bitter oranges to the Middle East.

Although they tasted sour, they were rich in vitamin C and contained almost as much pectin as quince.

Following the Arab trade routes, the trees eventually found their way to Spain, where they took root and flourished. When the fruit was exported to England, they became known as Seville oranges, after the city near where they were grown.

*I*n Spain, quince paste was called *membrillo*; and in Portugal, they made a solid version of it called *marmalada*.

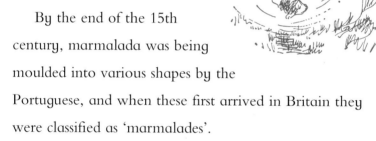

By the end of the 15th century, marmalada was being moulded into various shapes by the Portuguese, and when these first arrived in Britain they were classified as 'marmalades'.

Mr Gruber smiled when he saw me licking my lips. 'Not all history is dull, Mr Brown,' he said.

'It doesn't sound much like real marmalade to me, Mr Gruber,' I said.

'These so-called marmalades were often served at the end of a meal,' said Mr Gruber. 'They were cut into slices so that they could be eaten with the fingers. Until then,' he continued, 'honey was the only source of sweetening.'

'I'm glad I wasn't a bee in those days, Mr Gruber,' I said. 'They must have been kept very busy.'

'Perhaps that's where the phrase "busy bee" comes from,' said Mr Gruber. 'But all that was to change with the arrival on the scene of refined sugar. Being virtually flavourless, it was ideal for the making of jams and jellies.'

Another thing Mr Gruber told me was that in 1552, a French doctor and gifted prophet, who went under the name of Nostradamus, published a book of recipes. In it there was one for making a clear quince jelly, and another for preserving quartered bitter oranges which he said was, 'exceptionally delicious and good'.

Mr Damus isn't the only one who can see into the future. Bears are good at it too. Mr Gruber was so busy talking he didn't notice the cocoa was about to boil over. He was very pleased when I warned him.

*I*n 1561, Mary Queen of Scots was feeling seasick on a journey home from France, so she called for some marmalade, hoping it would make her feel better.

I think it probably helped because I was once taken out on the canoe lake at Southsea and the water was so choppy I had to have several marmalade sandwiches before I got my sea legs.

I was wondering why the man in charge kept calling out, 'Come in number nine' when I hadn't even gone anywhere.

*K*ing Henry VIII is said to have taken delivery of a whole case of marmalade. I can believe that too. Even if he was a king, anyone who had six wives must have needed all that marmalade to get through the day.

I think history is very interesting. So much of it happened before my time.

Over the next two centuries, people experimented with new ways of doing things, especially in matters to do with food, and early English cookery books began to have recipes for making marmalade using Seville oranges.

By 1861, Mrs Beeton, who was famous for her book of Household Management, had only one recipe for quince marmalade, but four for orange marmalade.

*T*he United Kingdom
in particular took
marmalade to its heart
and began exporting
it all over the world.

By the early 1900s, the Empress of Russia was receiving
regular supplies, and in 1911, Captain Scott took a tin of
it on his expedition to the North Pole.

Sir Winston Churchill was passionate about marmalade.
He said that along with bacon and eggs, it was an essential
part of English breakfast.

Mr Gruber, who also likes putting it on top of his bacon,
agrees with me that it probably helped Mr Churchill win
the war.

*B*y the end of
the 20th century,
there were lots of
large firms making
marmalade and
variations in flavour
sprang up as other
ingredients, ranging from
sweet oranges to apples, limes, whisky, even turnips and carrots,
were added to it.

Soon there were so many types of marmalade that the
European government issued a definitive ruling: *real* marmalade
must be made with citrus fruit.

'I do like a story with a happy ending,' said Mr Gruber.

A note from *M*r *G*ruber

If any reader of Mr Brown's book is interested in tasting quince paste, Juliet Kindersley of Sheepdrove Farm, Lambourne, makes it every October from fruit grown on the Kindersley's farm in the Ibiza area of Spain. Using organic sugar with no artificial flavouring or colouring, it is to be recommended.

*Visit **www.sheepdrove.com** to find out more.*

Marmalade Facts

Mr Gruber has kindly let me use his reference books, so here are some things you might like to know.

In 2007, the world's most expensive marmalade was produced by F. Duerr & Son to celebrate their 125th anniversary.

It was made from the finest Seville oranges, vintage whisky and more than a splash or two of Sir Winston Churchill's favourite vintage Champagne. It was then sprinkled with 24 carat gold flakes, so it's no wonder it wasn't cheap.

A small jar of it was valued at between £300 and £400, and it was calculated that the cost of covering a slice of toast worked out at £76. It sounds much too good to eat. I think I shall stick to my usual.

*I*n Italy there is a range of mountains called the Dolomites. They contain a lot of different coloured crystals known as dolomite, after an 18th century French explorer called Déodat de Dolomieu. The highest point is over 10,000 ft and it's called *Mount Marmolada*.

Seaside holidays are nice, but one day I wouldn't mind going there instead. If they have mineral deposits they might have marmalade ones too. Mr Brown thinks that even if they didn't before I arrived, they certainly would by the time I left!

On the 18th February 2007, the world's first ever Marmalade Festival took place at Dalemain, a manor house near Penrith in the Lake District of Cumbria.

There were talks and cookery demonstrations and free all-day breakfasts, not to mention face painting and stories for children.

The highlight was a marmalade tasting competition. With over 350 entries from all over the world, it took the judges almost 10 hours to taste them all. If you ask me, one good bear could have done it in half the time!

Q. What's square and white outside, orange inside, and can travel at over 100 miles an hour?

A. A train-driver's marmalade sandwich!

I thought that up last night while I was trying to get to sleep and it made me laugh so much Mrs Brown rushed in to see what all the fuss was about.

Marmalade Dos and Don'ts

*I*f you keep a marmalade sandwich under your hat in case of an emergency, *do* be very careful when you raise it. People not only give you funny looks; you may get pecked by a passing bird (Trafalgar Square is the worst place for this)!

If you take a book out of a library, *don't* use a chunk to mark something special. Librarians are funny people. You'd think they would be pleased that you didn't turn the corner of the page down.

*I*f you visit a maze, *do* make sure you leave a marmalade chunk every time you turn a corner. If you get lost you can always find your way out again and have a snack at the same time.

On the other hand, if you get taken to the theatre and sit in a front row upstairs or in a box, *don't* leave a marmalade sandwich on the ledge in front of you.

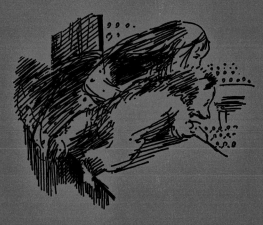

I did, and it fell on a man's head during an exciting part of a play. I didn't like to ask for it back before the end.

*I*f you are in a car and the driver gets lost, *don't* offer to look at the map.

Maps never say where you are, and by the time you've found out, it's too late because you've gone past wherever it was! Also, the place you are going to is always on the next page, so you need some way of marking the spot before you get to it.

Mr Brown grabbed the map from me one day and followed a marmalade chunk for several miles thinking it was a motorway. We ended up in a ploughed field and he wasn't best pleased!

$\mathcal{P}$ersonally, I've always found marmalade very useful for DIY. For instance, if you happen to saw a dining-room table in half by mistake, rubbing marmalade into the join works wonders. But make sure the curtains are drawn before you leave!

*I*f you get invited to a ball, *do* get your toenails cut, and *do* leave any marmalade sandwiches behind before you dance with the hostess.

I was dancing whilst carrying a book of instructions Mr Gruber had lent me and I couldn't really help getting my claws entangled with Mrs Smith Cholmley's shoe straps, especially as I was trying to stop a marmalade chunk falling down the back of her dress. I don't blame her for trying to escape – I was too!

Since I went to live with the Browns at number 32 Windsor Gardens, I have been lucky enough to test lots of different marmalades. (Mr Gruber says 'It's a hard job, but someone has to do it!')

In the end I think Mrs Bird's is the best of all. I like it because you are in charge of the chunks and can make them whatever size you like.

Mrs Bird has never written the recipe down because she does it all by feel, but as I am not allowed to do that she has agreed to dictate it to me, so here goes…

Mrs Bird's Marmalade Recipe

Adult supervision needed for all stages

You will need:

❋ 2lbs (0.9kg) Seville oranges, clean and free of blemishes, with thick, soft skins

❋ One lemon

❋ 4lbs (1.8kg) granulated sugar

❋ A saucepan large enough to hold 4 pints (2.3 litres) of water and the oranges

❋ A sharp knife, chopping board, wooden spoon and a ladle

❋ A muslin bag for the pips

❋ A supply of clean screw top jars and some waxed paper circles to fit

N.B. Seville oranges arrive early in the year, so make sure you buy them in good time.

1. Wash the fruit and place it in the saucepan along with the water.
2. Bring to the boil and let it simmer for long enough to soften the fruit.
3. Lower the heat, remove the fruit, and when cool enough to handle, cut it into quarters.
4. Remove the pips and put them into the muslin bag.
5. Squeeze the juice into the saucepan of water.
6. Slice the peel into strips, thick or thin as you prefer, and add them and the bag of pips to the saucepan.
7. Note the level of the water and turn up the heat again until it boils.

8. Allow the water to slow boil for an hour or so until the contents have been reduced by about a third.

9. Remove the bag of pips, then pour in the sugar and bring to the boil again. A little lemon juice added at this stage will give it a sparkle and help it to set.

10. Stir constantly until the sugar has dissolved, then leave it to simmer.

11. Keep a watchful eye on the mixture until it begins to darken.

12. In the meantime sterilize the jars with hot water and leave them in a warm oven.

13. To test the consistency of the marmalade, allow a drop to fall off the end of the spoon on to a cold plate. It should begin to set almost immediately.

Mrs Bird's Tip: Leave the marmalade for a moment or two before poking it with your index finger. The surface should wrinkle. If it tastes too sweet add some lemon juice. If it is too sharp try adding a little sugar.

P.S. That's something else I'm not allowed to do, which is a pity because bears are good at that kind of thing!

14. Using the ladle, begin filling the jars.
As soon as each one is full, place a paper
disc on top, waxed surface downwards,
making sure there are no air pockets.
Leave to cool before screwing the lids
on tightly.

Mrs Bird's Tip: A wide-necked funnel helps with the pouring.

Paddington's Tip: If there is any left over, don't throw it away. There are all sorts of different ways of using it up.

$\mathcal{M}$rs Bird often mixes her leftover marmalade with an equal amount of golden syrup, adds some lemon juice and water and puts it on to boil, stirring all the time. It makes a very tasty pancake filling, but don't try it on Shrove Tuesday when you toss them. It takes a long time removing them from the ceiling!

A lot of cookery books use marmalade in their recipes. Mrs Beeton had one for a marmalade and vermicelli pudding, and a famous French chef, Paul Bocuse, has a recipe for bread and butter pudding with a layer of orange marmalade.

Since I have been living with the Browns, Mrs Bird has been using more and more marmalade. She collects a lot when she cleans out my jars to save me using my paws, so here are a few more ideas for using it up:

In the winter try making steamed suet dumplings with a marmalade filling instead of jam. It's also very good in cakes, and a layer of it inside a home-made chocolate cake makes a big difference.

$\mathcal{N}$owadays, especially in Scotland, you can even buy marmalade ice cream, and in Sweden they eat it with their cheese.

Mrs Bird often mixes in a dessert spoonful or two when she is making an apple flan. (Or three if I'm helping!) It's also very good in rice pudding.

I think if I was a chef, I might put marmalade with lots of different things – just to see what happens. You don't know until you try!

Removing Marmalade Stains

Eating toast and marmalade isn't as easy as it sounds, especially with paws. Marmalade drips through the holes. Bears don't often wear a tie so most of it goes on my duffle coat.

Mrs Bird's Method

❋ First of all, scrape as much off as you can with a blunt knife.

❋ If cold water doesn't work, try making up a mixture of white vinegar to which a little borax powder and some salt has been added. Dab it on the affected area, then wash clean.

N.B. If the fabric is brightly coloured, always try it out on an inconspicuous area first in case the dye runs.

$\mathcal{A}$unt $\mathcal{L}$ucy's $\mathcal{M}$ethod

They don't have much money in the Home for Retired Bears in Lima, so they have to make do the best they can.

Aunt Lucy says removing stains needs plenty of elbow grease. Unfortunately, because bears elbows are covered in fur, they get very dry, so she often used to put my duffle coat on to boil in a giant cauldron they have.

All the other bears agreed it made a lovely soup. They called it 'Aunt Lucy's Allsorts' – they never knew what was coming next.

$\mathcal{M}$any people claim to have invented marmalade, but it's impossible to credit any one person. All that can be said is that it began somewhere in Greece several thousand years ago when someone with an enquiring mind split open a quince to see what was inside.

Others have brought their ideas to bear on it over the years, and it just grew and grew. To all those who helped it on its way, we marmalade lovers can only say *'thank you'*. Breakfast wouldn't be the same without it. *P.B.*

$\mathcal{A}$ $\mathcal{T}$hank you from the $\mathcal{A}$uthor

I would like to thank the following for their help in preparing this book:

❁ Mr Gruber, for his historical facts and figures

❁ Mrs Bird, for her marmalade recipe

❁ Mr Brown, for the use of his computer

(I hope the makers return it soon. Mrs Brown is quite right when she says marking the pop-out drawer in the front 'DVD' is asking for trouble. They should have a notice saying 'NOT TO BE USED FOR MARMALADE SANDWICHES'. How was I to know?)

❁ Mr Bond, for the loan of his screwdriver

More Paddington titles to collect

FICTION

Paddington Here and Now
HB ISBN: 978-0-00-726940-2
CD ISBN: 978-0-00-727086-6

A Bear Called Paddington
HB ISBN: 978-0-00-714187-6
PB ISBN: 978-0-00-717416-4
CD ISBN: 978-0-00-716165-2

More About Paddington
PB ISBN: 978-0-00-675343-8
CD ISBN: 978-0-00-716168-3

Paddington Abroad
PB ISBN: 978-0-00-777022-9

Paddington At Large
PB ISBN: 978-0-00-675363-6

Paddington At Work
PB ISBN: 978-0-00-675367-4

Paddington Goes to Town
PB ISBN: 978-0-00-675366-7

Paddington Helps Out
PB ISBN: 978-0-00-675344-5

Paddington Marches On
PB ISBN: 978-0-00-675362-9

Paddington On Top
PB ISBN: 978-0-00-675377-3

Paddington Takes the Air
PB ISBN: 978-0-00-675379-7

Paddington Takes the Test
PB ISBN: 978-0-00-675378-0

PICTURE BOOKS